UP A TREE

by Rick Watson   illustrated by Constance Bergum

SCHOLASTIC INC.
New York   Toronto   London   Auckland   Sydney
Mexico City   New Delhi   Hong Kong   Buenos Aires

Developed by Kirchoff/Wohlberg, Inc., in cooperation with Scholastic Inc.

5 6 7 8 9 10   08   09 08 07 06

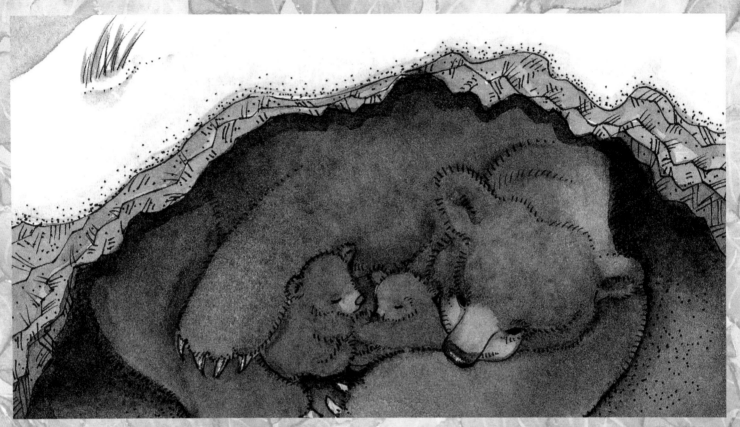

These bear cubs were born last winter in a cozy cave.
It snowed outside for months, and Momma Bear slept the whole time. The cubs stayed warm, though. They curled up in their mother's fur. When Momma Bear woke up, she nuzzled her little cubs and bathed them with her scratchy tongue.

Momma Bear was happy to see her cubs, but she was also very hungry. She had not eaten a bite in almost five months! She went outside to look for food.

The two cubs had never been outside. The girl cub ran and jumped. She wanted to play. The boy cub was very shy. He stayed close to his mother's side.

3

The cubs tried to play with some of the other animals in the forest. The other animals didn't want to play. The birds flew into the sky. The rabbits ran into the bushes. The moles dug into the ground.

Before long, the climbing lessons began. The girl cub scooted right up the tree trunk. She even crawled out onto a limb.

4

The boy cub climbed only halfway up. Momma Bear scolded him, "Climb higher!" she grunted. "This may save you when there is danger." He slowly climbed to the top. "Good. Now come down," grunted Momma Bear.

The girl cub tried to climb past her brother, but she slipped and went tumbling down. The boy cub fell, too. Then they both climbed back up. After a while they got very good at climbing.

One day, the bear cubs were fishing in the stream. The girl cub wanted to wrestle. She splashed water all over her brother. Soon, they were rolling around in the mud.

Suddenly, Momma Bear grunted a warning. The cubs ran to the nearest pine tree. They climbed up as fast as they could. Then they saw the trouble—a mountain lion!

Momma Bear stood on her back legs. She raised
her big paws and growled. Momma Bear swiped at
the mountain lion until the big cat finally ran away.

In autumn, the leaves turned bright colors. The little cubs had grown. They still had many lessons to learn, though.

One day, the girl cub chased an animal. The animal was black with a white stripe. It ran into a hollow log to hide from her. The cub pushed her nose into the log and grunted. She was just being friendly.

The little animal in the log was a skunk. He thought that the bear cub wanted to eat him, so he squirted a smelly spray in her face! She smelled like a skunk for weeks!

By winter, the cubs had grown fat. They were also very, very sleepy. They crawled into their cave with Momma Bear and fell asleep. They slept and slept and slept and slept. The bears didn't eat or drink all winter. Their bodies used their fat for food. Their thick fur kept them warm.

When the bears woke up, it was spring. Momma Bear knew that soon it would be time to leave her cubs alone.

The bear cubs were fully grown by summer. One day, they found a beehive. They knew that it was filled with honey. They loved honey, but they didn't like bees. "Momma Bear isn't afraid of bees," they thought. "We can ask her to get the honey for us."

When the cubs got home, they went fishing. Momma Bear stood very still in the water, but there were no fish for her to catch. They were going to tell her about the hive when Momma Bear grunted a loud warning. "Hurry," she warned them. "Up that tree!"

It was time for her cubs to become adults.

Momma Bear grunted one last time, "Stay!" Then she walked off into the forest.

They sat down on a branch to wait. They waited and waited and waited.

The bear cubs soon grew tired of waiting. They tried to wrestle, but almost fell. They tried to catch some dragonflies, but the big bugs flew out of reach. They tried swapping places in the tree.

They were hungry, their bellies rumbled. Momma Bear did not come back.

Before long, the sun set behind the hills. The forest became dark and quiet. The cubs could barely see each other. They had never been alone at night.

13

At sunrise, the cubs were still awake. They were still hungry! They saw other animals eating breakfast. "Let's go find some food," grunted the boy bear. "Momma Bear told us to stay here. She might be mad," the girl bear grunted.

Her brother was already scooting down the tree. Then her belly rumbled again. "Hey! Wait for me!" she grunted.

The boy bear led his sister to the beehive. The hive hung high in an oak tree. It was dripping with sweet honey, but angry bees buzzed all around the hive. They wanted to protect the hive from the bears.

"I wish Momma was here," grunted the girl bear. "She would get us some honey to eat." Just then, the boy bear stood up on his back legs. He looked bigger than ever before. He swatted at the hive with his paws. The bees stung his nose and his ears, but his thick fur protected him.

The two bears sat on a log and ate honey. They forgot all about bee stings. They even ate some bees with the honey. Then the girl bear tried to lick a drop of honey from one of the boy bear's ears. It tickled! Soon they were wrestling in the dirt. They felt full and happy and playful.

Momma Bear had taught them well. They would be able to help each other for a while. They weren't little cubs now. They were almost grown. They went off to go fishing.